This book is in memory of Fr. Bede Scholz, O.S.B.,
who for years wanted me to do a book for children about angels!

I'd also like to thank Margaret, Cecilia, Gina and Katrina D.,
who took the "puzzle" and put it together.

G. P. PUTNAM'S SONS
A division of Penguin Young Readers Group
Published by The Penguin Group
Penguin Group (USA) Inc., 375 Hudson Street, New York, NY 10014, U.S.A.
Penguin Group (Canada), 10 Alcorn Avenue, Toronto, Ontario, Canada M4V 3B2 (a division of Pearson Penguin Canada Inc.).
Penguin Books Ltd, 80 Strand, London WC2R 0RL, England.
Penguin Ireland, 25 St. Stephen's Green, Dublin 2, Ireland (a division of Penguin Books Ltd.).
Penguin Group (Australia), 250 Camberwell Road, Camberwell, Victoria 3124, Australia (a division of Pearson Australia Group Pty Ltd).
Penguin Books India Pvt Ltd, 11 Community Centre, Panchsheel Park, New Delhi - 110 017, India.
Penguin Group (NZ), Cnr Airborne and Rosedale Roads, Albany, Auckland 1310, New Zealand (a division of Pearson New Zealand Ltd).
Penguin Books (South Africa) (Pty) Ltd, 24 Sturdee Avenue, Rosebank, Johannesburg 2196, South Africa.
Penguin Books Ltd, Registered Offices: 80 Strand, London WC2R 0RL, England.

Manufactured in China by South China Printing Co. Ltd. Design by Gina DiMassi.
Library of Congress Cataloging-in-Publication Data
De Paola, Tomie. Angels, angels everywhere / Tomie dePaola. p. cm. Summary: Illustrations depict the various types of angels that
take care of children in their everyday lives, such as The Wake-Up Angel, The Music Angel, and The Pajama and Bathrobe Angel.
[1. Angels—Fiction. 2. Day—Fiction.] I. Title. PZ7.D439Ao 2005 [E]—dc22 2004026987
ISBN 0-399-24370-4
1 3 5 7 9 10 8 6 4 2
First Impression

ANGELS, ANGELS EVERYWHERE

TOMIE dePAOLA

G. P. PUTNAM'S SONS
NEW YORK

THE · · WAKE · UP · ANGEL · · · · · · ·

THE · GET-DRESSED · ANGEL

THE · KITCHEN · ANGEL

·THE · SCHOOL · ANGEL · · ·

· · · · · THE · READING · ANGEL · · · · ·

THE · MUSIC · ANGEL

· · · · THE · ART · ANGEL · · · · ·

THE · PET · ANGEL ·

THE · PLAY · ANGELS

THE · GARDEN · ANGEL ·

THE · TEA · PARTY · ANGEL

THE · POPCORN · ANGEL

THE · BABYSITTING · ANGEL

· THE · · GUARDING · · ANGELS ·

THE · BATH · ANGEL

· · THE · PAJAMA · AND · BATHROBE · ANGEL · · ·

THE · GOODNIGHT · ANGEL